Aunt Nell's
Dandy
Duckling

A. L. Kirby

AUNT NELL'S

Dandy Duckling

A. L. KIRBY

Printed in the United States of America

ISBN: Softcover 978-1-964331-06-5
Publication Date: 10/04/2024

Dedication

Warmest thanks to my dear, long-time friend, Nell Parsons, for sharing her memories about raising an orphaned wild duckling. It has been great fun telling Nell's experience from her Ducky's point of view. May this small book bring lots of smiles to Nell's face and to the faces of children and kids-at-heart everywhere!

AUNT NELL'S
Dandy Duckling

(this story is based on real life events)

Chapter One
Breaking Free

My name is Dandy Duckling, but I like being called Ducky. This is because I have pleasant memories of the time when I was a tiny baby bird. Back then, Aunt Nell often picked me up, stroked my soft, little head and said, *Hi there Dandy Duckling. You are a very nice little Ducky. I'm happy I found you.*

At first I couldn't understand what Aunt Nell was saying, but it didn't take long for me to learn what some of her words meant. I tried very hard to respond to her, but no matter how hard I tried, I couldn't get the knack of speaking her language. The only sounds that ever came out of my mouth were lots of quacks! Sometimes I quacked quietly. Sometimes I quacked loudly. Once in a while, when I was excited, I quacked with a mixture of loud quacks, quiet quacks, and squeaky quacks. This always brought a smile to Aunt Nell's face. She smiled because she thought my quacking sounded musical and entertaining.

Even though I never learned to speak Aunt Nell's language, we communicated with each other quite well. I found it easy to understand her tone of voice. I could even sense her moods. If she was happy, she hummed a merry tune. If she was lonely, a few shiny tears would roll down her cheeks. When that happened, I would try to cheer her up by nibbling at her fingers and sometimes, I nibbled her ears.

It was fun living with Aunt Nell. I loved her and she loved me… and in my heart of hearts, even though we were as different as bugs are from frogs, I believed Aunt Nell was my mother.

But wait! If you are reading this story, you must be wondering how such a loving relationship developed between a duckling and a human lady. To help you understand how it did, I will start my story from its beginning:

My very first memory is of the time when I was living inside a shell. Back then, I didn't have a name. I didn't even know what a name was. In fact, I didn't know much of anything at all. This was because I started out as a wee speck of life inside a shell slowly developing into a tiny baby duckling.

It was warm and cozy inside the shell. I had lots of room to wiggle around inside the shell… or at least, at first I did. However, as each day passed, I kept growing larger. The bigger I got, the more squeezed and uncomfortable I became, until one day, I had grown so much I could hardly move around at all. When that happened, I thought to myself, *If I don't get out of this shell soon, I'm going to get squashed!*

I had a problem and I didn't know what to do to about it. I tried and tried to think of a way to get out of the shell, but I was stumped. I wanted to come up with an escape plan, but the more I tried to make a plan, the more puzzled and perplexed I became. This stressed me out, so I banged my bill as hard as I could against the shell… and CRAAACK!

The loud noise startled me. I was scared. I was so frightened I hunched down, closed my eyes, and shook like a leaf. I'm not sure how long I remained crouched in that position, but after a while, when nothing terrible happened, I slowly opened my eyes and glanced around.

Everything appeared to be the same as before, until I looked up. Much to my surprise, I saw a glimmering ray of sunlight shining through a small hole in top of the shell above my head. As I gazed at the hole, I could tell it was too small for me to squeeze through it and get out of the shell.

A wave of disappointment washed over me. If I stayed in the shell much longer, I knew I would be squished. I had to get out of it. But how was I going to do that?

As I sat there staring at the hole feeling sad, hopeless, and distressed, a bright idea flashed into my mind and I said to myself, maybe *if I keep on banging my bill against the shell as hard as I can, the opening will get bigger and I can escape.*

Trembling with excitement and filled with fresh determination, I started banging my bill against the shell.

I banged and I banged and I banged. I must have banged at least a hundred times before I became discouraged and stopped banging.

My efforts had not brought any results and I felt totally defeated. In fact, I had never felt more miserable. I was ready to give up trying to escape, when much to my surprise, I heard a clear voice speaking to me.

LITTLE DUCKLING, DON'T YOU DARE GIVE UP! IF AT FIRST YOU DON'T SUCCEED, TRY AGAIN, said the voice.

I looked around but nobody else was there. Where had the small voice come from? I was puzzled. I did not know what to think at first, but after awhile, I decided the voice I'd heard must have been the voice of my own little duck- heart speaking to me. Yes. I was certain it was, so I decided to follow my heart's advice and have another try at breaking the shell.

I mustered every bit of my remaining strength, leaned back and lunged forward as fast as I could. Then, as my little bill struck the shell… CRACK! CRACK! CRACK!

What a surprise! The shell had split wide open! I could hardly believe my eyes,

Hurray! Woo-hoo! Yippy! I'm free! I shouted with excitement.

As I stepped out over a whole bunch of busted pieces of shell into a fascinating, amazing, beautiful New World, my heart swelled with joy.

Chapter Two
From Here to There

Everything in this new-to-me place was far more wonderful than I could have ever imagined. Fluffy, snow-white clouds danced through the azure-blue sky. Emerald-green grass stretched out in front of me for as far as I could see. It felt wonderfully soft and comfortable beneath my little webbed feet.

As I waddled along, I saw lots of pieces of broken shell scattered here and there next to a nest on the ground and I said to myself, *It looks like some other ducklings broke through their shells before I broke through mine! If my guess is right and there really are other ducklings, most likely they have gone on a walk with my mother.*

I knew I belonged with my family, but I didn't know where to look for them.

The more I thought about this, the lonelier I became. Being lonely was not a good feeling. I had a painful lump in my throat and teardrops in my eyes. In spite of this, I decided to go searching for them.

I imagined how good it would feel when I found my mother and the other ducklings. Imagining this filled me with fresh hope and courage and I said, *I will find my family. I will search and search until I do! Nothing can stop me.*

So I walked. I walked for a long, long time. I searched all over but I couldn't find my mama or any other ducks at all.

Sharp pangs of loneliness stabbed at my heart. Unhappy thoughts flooded my mind and I felt completely discouraged. Feeling more blue and down than ever before, I said to myself, *No mama duck exists. There aren't any other ducklings either. I am all alone.*

In spite of feeling this way, I kept trudging along in the twilight looking here and there for my family. Finally I was too tired to go any further, so I sat down, leaned against a tree, and fell asleep. I slept soundly until a beam of sunlight shining in my face awakened me.

Although my heart was still heavy and I had almost given up hope of finding my family, I continued my search. I trudged along looking here and there until I saw something rushing toward me. I didn't know what it was. I wondered if it might be my mother and a glimmer of hope rose up in my heart, so I ran forward to greet whoever it was.

While racing forward, I thought to myself, *Every duckling that ever hatched has a mother somewhere! That's got to be my mother! I can hardly wait to meet her.*

As I neared the stranger, I could see it was way too big to be a mama duck. In fact, it didn't look like a duck at all. It had four legs instead of two! It had a mouth and a nose on a muzzle instead of a beautiful bill like mine… and it was covered with fur instead of feathers.

WOOF! GRRR! YAP! GRRR! BOW WOW! YAP! GRRR! WOOF! GRRR!

When I heard the weird noises the creature was making, I was scared. I wanted to turn around and run, but I couldn't move. All I could do was stand in the same spot quivering and shaking like I was frozen there.

As soon as the whatever-it-was reached me, it picked me up in its huge, slippery, slobbery mouth and threw me high into the air. I didn't know what was happening. Was this strange, ferocious beast going to eat me? Was I going to be its lunch?

Each time the creature hurled me up into the air, as I fell back toward the ground, it caught me again in its horrible mouth. After that, it tossed me high again. I can't remember how many times this happened, but I do recall wishing it would stop. But it didn't stop. Instead, it kept throwing me high in the air over and over again. I was terrified but I was too shocked and weak to do anything except go limp.

If Aunt Nell had not been looking out the window of her cozy country home at that specific time, this horrifying incident would likely have been the end of me. I don't think I could have survived much longer. Thank goodness, when Aunt Nell saw what her dog was doing, she hurried from the house to check things out.

What in the world is my mischievous Puppy up to? said Aunt Nell to herself, as she ran toward her dog. It looks like Puppy is tossing something around. If it's a rock, she might choke on it. A rock could break some of Puppy's teeth.

When Puppy heard her name being called, she came running toward her mistress and dropped me from her wet, slobbery mouth at Aunt Nell's feet.

Aunt Nell was shocked to see me lying there like a limp rag. I was all slimy and dripping wet from being in the dog's mouth. I did not look pretty at all, but this did not stop Aunt Nell from reaching down and picking me up.

Aunt Nell's Dandy Duckling

Oh, you poor little duckling, said Aunt Nell, as she examined me. You look dreadful. Your downy coat is all slippery and gooey, but I don't think you are seriously injured. Being tossed around like a ball must have been a dreadful experience. You look terribly lost and lonely, but don't worry. I'll take care of you. I'll make sure you survive.

Or at least, I think that's what Aunt Nell said, because back then, I couldn't understand people-talk very well.

It felt wonderful to still be alive and I was grateful because, even though I hadn't found my mother or my brothers and sisters, I had found somebody who loved me. Yes, all was good and deep in my little duck heart-of-hearts, I knew everything was going to be okay.

Chapter Three
The Old Tin Laundry Tub

After gently stroking my head, Aunt Nell carried me into her garage, put me into an old tin laundry tub and said, *I know you are starving-hungry but I don't have any duckling food. I will go to the feed store and buy something for you to eat. You will be safe in the laundry tub while I'm away. I will be back in half an hour.*

While Aunt Nell was away, I paced back and forth from one end of the laundry tub to the other. I didn't like being in the laundry tub. Being in that old tin thing felt even worse than when I was tightly crammed into an eggshell!

My tummy rumbled. I was growing hungrier by the minute and was in a grumpy mood. I asked myself why Aunt Nell was taking such a long time? When was she coming back? If she didn't get back soon, I was going to collapse. I wondered how long I could stay alive if I collapsed.

At the very moment I was thinking these dismal thoughts, the garage door opened and in walked Aunt Nell carrying a bulky bag.

Hello Ducky, said Aunt Nell cheerfully, I brought you something nice.

Aunt Nell took two little ceramic bowls out of the bag and placed them side by side in the tub. She filled one of the bowls with water and filled the other bowl with a mealy, golden-brown substance.

Filled with curiosity, I waddled over to the bowl filled with the mealy stuff and took a big bite of it.

Aurgchch! Aurgchch! Cough! Cough! Cough! Cough!

Much to my horror, I was choking. I could hardly breathe at all.

When Aunt Nell saw what was happening, she reached down into the other bowl and splashed some water onto my bill. I opened my bill wide, swallowed, and thankfully, quit choking!

Dear Ducky, said Aunt Nell sympathetically, You must learn to take a drink of water with your food. The water will wash the food down and you won't choke. I caught on quickly and, after that, I was careful to drink a little water while eating duck meal and I never choked again.

After I finished my first meal, my tummy was full and I felt much better. However, I was still tired and I couldn't stop yawning. In fact, I was so tired, I could hardly keep my eyes open.

When Aunt Nell noticed my eyes fluttering, she took a small, soft blanket out of her bag and placed it in a corner of the tub. She lifted me gently onto the blanket and said, *Dear little Ducky, it's time for you to go to sleep. I hope you have a good rest. I'll be back in the morning.*

I snuggled deep down into the warmth of the blanket and the last thing I heard was Aunt Nell's footsteps, as she walked out of the garage and closed the door.

Chapter Four
To Find of Not to Find

Early the next morning, the garage door opened and in walked Aunt Nell. After greeting me with a smile, she filled my water bowl with fresh water and my feed bowl with delicious duckling food. I started eating right away. I didn't choke because I remembered to chug down some water along with my feed.

When I finished eating, Aunt Nell told me she would be taking me on a treasure hunt. She said the treasure we would be looking for was my mother and my brothers and sisters.

It will be exciting to meet your family, said Aunt Nell, as she picked me up, placed me in her shirt pocket, and walked outside.

That day Aunt Nell walked for a long way with me in her pocket. Puppy (the dog that had tossed me around) and Puppy's mother, a friendly pooch called Whitey, followed close behind us. At first, I was afraid of Aunt Nell's pets, but I gradually overcame my fear and once in a while, I poked my head out of the pocket to see what the dogs were doing. It amused me to see them romping around together and I secretly wished I could be down there playing with them.

An hour passed before we came to a familiar-looking location. I knew it was the place where I had broken out the shell because, as I gazed around, I recognized the egg shells I had noticed shortly after I left my shell. While I was looking at the shells, Aunt Nell took me out of her pocket and set me on the grass.

After Aunt Nell carefully examined the shells, she said, *I think this is the place where you hatched. I believe your brother and sister ducklings hatched here too. They probably hatched a day or two earlier than you did, but since you were still in your shell, you couldn't go with them when Mother Duck led them away. Mother Duck likely took them to a pond and right now, your mother and her ducklings are very likely splashing around in the water having a good time. Let's go find them!*

I liked Aunt Nell's idea. I was eager to find my family and when Aunt Nell started walking through the lush, green grass, I waddled along behind her quacking happily.

After a while, we came to a place where there was a lot of water and I politely asked Aunt Nell if this was the pond my Mama and her ducklings were swimming in.

Aunt Nell must have understood what I said, because she nodded and smiled. With me following behind her, Aunt Nell walked the entire perimeter of the pond. She looked at the pond from every angle but neither of us saw any ducks. We searched through the reeds surrounding the pond, but there weren't any ducks there. No matter how hard we searched, we did not find my family. In fact, we did not even see a duck feather!

In spite of our disappointment, Aunt Nell was determined to keep looking for my family. She told me there was another pond in the area, so we went to it too.

By the time Aunt Nell and I reached the other pond, we were growing tired, but we did not give up. While we were there, we continued searching but we couldn't find any ducks at that pond either. I was disappointed. My head hung low and teardrops fell from my eyes.

When Aunt Nell saw my tears, she picked me up, cuddled me close to her chest and said, *I am sorry we were not able to find your mother and her ducklings. I know how awful you feel. Being tired, sad, hungry, and discouraged isn't any fun at all, but don't worry. When we get back home, I'll take care for you.*

When we got back to Aunt Nell's home, the sun was going down. It had been a long day and, once again I was very hungry and very sleepy. I was glad when Aunt Nell took me into the garage, put me in the laundry tub and gave me some duckling food.

After eating my fill, I paced back and forth in the tub thinking about how disappointed I was. I felt like a failure, so I looked up at Aunt Nell and stomped one of my little webbed feet.

When Aunt Nell saw me stomping, she said, *I know you are disappointed we didn't find your family. On top of that, I am certain you don't like staying in this old laundry tub. It is too small for you to feel at home in. When tomorrow comes, I'm going to give you a big surprise. You will like it a lot. It will help you feel better.*

Chapter Five
The Big Surprise

After a long, sound sleep, a sunbeam shined in through the garage window and awakened me. I yawned and looked around hoping to see Aunt Nell, but she wasn't there.

I was hungry and my empty tummy was rumbling. I waddled over and looked in my feed bowl, but it was empty. Lucky for me, there was some water in the other bowl. After taking a big drink, I felt better, but my stomach was still feeling uncomfortable.

Where was Aunt Nell? Why wasn't she here? I was annoyed. Frankly, I was also so cranky I let out the loudest series of **QUACK-QUACK- QUACKS** a duckling has ever made.

Aunt Nell must have heard me, because a few minutes later, she came into the garage and said, *Hi Ducky. I hope you slept well. You must be hungry.*

Aunt Nell re-filled my feed dish and, after she did, she told me to eat up and reminded me not to forget to take a drink of water with each mouthful. I was careful to follow her directions and I didn't even choke once.

After I finished eating, I looked up at Aunt Nell with questioning eyes and asked, *Where is my surprise?*

I'm sure Aunt Nell understood what I said, because she picked me up and carried me outside to a big horse watering trough.

This is your surprise, said Aunt Nell. It's your new home. You will have much more room to waddle around in this trough than you did in that old tin laundry tub. I put some water in the bottom of this trough. You will be able to learn to swim in it!

When Aunt Nell set me down on the platform inside the trough, I felt like I was an explorer on a great adventure. I was eager to make many important discoveries, so I waddled around on the platform investigating every inch of it. As I walked around, I discovered a match box filled with duckling feed and a container filled with water (but I wasn't hungry or thirsty, so I didn't stop to sample them.) Instead, I continued checking things out and as I did, I discovered a small wooden box filled with fresh hay. I liked the smell of the hay, so I hopped up onto it and took several deep whiffs. The hay felt nice and soft beneath my feet as I snuggled down into it, but I only stayed there for a minute before I jumped from the hay, ran to the front edge of the platform and looked down at the water in the bottom of the trough. As I stared at the water, it seemed to call out to me and a strange longing filled my heart. I yearned to walk down the ramp and splash in the water, but the ramp seemed too steep for me to safely walk on it. What would happen if I swayed too much while I was walking down it? If I took a tumble and rolled down the ramp, I might get hurt. I had experienced a lot of trauma in the past few days and I didn't have much self confidence left. If the truth be told, I was afraid to attempt doing something dangerous. So I turned around and strolled back and forth and back and forth from one end of the platform to the other end. I tried to work up the courage to walk down the ramp but I did not succeed. I wondered why I wasn't brave enough to give it a try?

I wished Aunt Nell would pick me up and put me down into the water instead of just standing there watching me pace. To express my wish, I made several kinds of quacking sounds, but she didn't seem to understand what I was saying.

I said to myself, *Aunt Nell thinks I'm a big sissy. She thinks I am scared to walk down the ramp, but I'm not. I will prove to her I am a brave little duckling.*

To show Aunt Nell I was brave enough to walk down the ramp and get into the water, I carefully placed my right foot on the ramp. I wanted to put my left foot on the ramp too, but instead of placing it there, I trembled and did not move my left foot.

C'mon, Ducky, don't be scared. You can do it, said Aunt Nell.

I appreciated Aunt Nell's encouragement and I knew if I didn't put my left foot on the ramp soon, I probably never would. As I stood there trying to work up the courage to pput both feet on the ramp, I grew dizzy. I knew if I stood in that position any longer, I would lose my balance and take a tumble. I didn't want to fall, so I swallowed hard, took a deep breath, and placed my left foot onto the ramp with my right one.

I was so proud of myself! I looked up at Aunt Nell and shouted, WOO-HOO-KOO-QUACK… or something like that! Then I wobbled carefully down the ramp and, before I knew it, I had reached its bottom and was splashing in the water!

Feeling happy as could be, I waved my wee wings rapidly back and called out QUACKOO-QUACKOO-QUACKOO (which in duckling talk meant I was really, really, really excited because now I was swimming!)

Swimming had come naturally to me and I liked it a lot. I swam back and forth and around and around in circles. Once in a while, I stopped long enough to waddle up the ramp and take a few bites of duckling feed, but I didn't stop up top for long. Soon I hurried back down and continued playing.

I was having so much fun, I lost track of time and, before I knew it, the sun was going down. When I looked around, I discovered Aunt Nell was no longer standing nearby watching me. I didn't know where she had gone or why she had left without saying goodbye. I wished Aunt Nell had taken me with her.

I flapped my little wings and shouted, *Aunt Nell, Aunt Nell, come back* (but I yelled it in duckling talk, so even if Aunt Nell had heard me, she probably would not have understood what QUACK-QUICK- QUICK-QUACK meant.)

I was hungry and tired, so I ate my duckling food. To be safe, I took several sips of water along with it. Everything was good. Except for being tired and exhausted, I felt fine, so I hopped up onto the hay and fell fast asleep.

The next morning, as the day began to dawn, I was awakened by a very loud YIPPITY YAP! YIPPITY! YIPPITY! YIPPITY YAP!

When I looked up, I saw a scary, large, dark shape soaring through the air above the trough. As the shape swooped toward the trough, Aunt Nell's dog Whitey, who had been guarding the trough while I slept, barked more loudly and fiercely than ever and, when she did, the large bird turned tail and flew away.

I sighed with relief. I was thankful Whitey had seen the large bird swooping toward the trough and her noisy barking had frightened the fearful thing away. Whitey's shrill bark had also awakened Aunt Nell.

When Aunt Nell heard the noise, she came running outside to see what was happening.

Upon reaching the trough, Aunt Nell patted Whitey's head and said, *Good dog, Thank you for guarding the trough and keeping Ducky safe. If that eagle would have swooped down, picked up Ducky and carried her away, poor Ducky would have been its breakfast.*

After speaking these words, Aunt Nell carried me back into the garage. Once there, she put me into the old tin laundry tub. By then, I had stopped shaking and somehow, being in the tub felt good. I was thankful to be safe again.

Chapter Six

Safety First

I remember feeling annoyed with Aunt Nell for leaving me in the laundry tub for long periods of time, so one day I pretended to be asleep when she came to check on me.

Hi Ducky, said Aunt Nell cheerfully. *I had a busy morning trying to think of a way to make sure you stay safe when you are outside in the trough. I spent several hours wracking my brain pondering how to keep prowling coyotes, wolves, foxes, and birds of prey from devouring you when you are in there. Thank goodness I managed to come up with an idea.*

Aunt Nell went on to tell me she had put a chain link panel over most of the top of the trough. After that, she had placed a wooden plank over the open part of the panel. She explained she could open and close the lid when she put me out of or into the trough. She told me, from now on, I would be safe when I was in the trough and I didn't need to worry anymore about something unfortunate happening to me.

While Aunt Nell was assuring me of my safety, Whitey stood nearby wagging her tail. Whitey seemed to have understood what Aunt Nell said, because after that, she didn't stay quite as close to the trough, though she was still protective of me and always chased Puppy away when Puppy came too close to me. I wondered if this was because Whitey remembered how Puppy had tossed me into the air like a ball and she did not want that to happen again!

I remember how, when Aunt Nell's curious horses walked up to the trough and poked their noses at the chain link covering, Whitey would chase them away. Aunt Nell had laughed when she saw Whitey guarding me from the horses. Whitey's courage pleased and amused her.

Although I was usually happy when I was in the trough, once in a while, a strange, feeling washed over me. When this happened, I knew something was missing from my life. But I didn't know what it was, so I would pout and stand in the same spot for a long, long time trying to figure why I felt so blue. One day, while I was standing staring at the trough walls feeling sad, Aunt Nell walked up to the trough and said, *Ducky, you are looking gloomy today. Would you like to go for walk around the yard with me?*

I looked up at Aunt Nell and said, *Quackedy, quackedy, quackedy, quick* (which in duck talk meant: Of course I would. I would really, really love to walk around the entire acreage with you.)

From then on, Whitey and Puppy and I followed Aunt Nell around her farmyard almost every day. It was good to be out and about in the fresh air and sunshine, though, at first, some of the new sights frightened me.

I didn't like Aunt Nell's hens and her rooster really gave me the he- be-jeebies. I tried to avoid them until the day I saw a fat hen strutting around near the chicken coop with several cute, fluffy chicks following her. I thought the chicks would make wonderful playmates, so I hurried toward them. When the hen saw me coming, she ran toward me clucking loudly. She flapped her wings so wildly it scared me and I ran away from her as fast as I could. From then on, I minded my own business and never tried to befriend any chicks again!

Whitey continued to be a wonderful guardian. She kept me from getting into a lot of trouble. I remember the day when Casper, Aunt Nell's green-eyed, black cat came close to me and hunched his back. He was about to pounce on me and scratch me with his long, sharp claws, when Whitey saw him and chased him away. Another time, when I was strolling through a nearby field, Aunt Nell's horses came close and tried to nibble my downy back, but Whitey ran toward the horses barking loudly. When she reached the horses, Whitey nipped at their heels and they galloped away. The horses stayed clear of me after that. Thank goodness, they never tried to nibble on me again.

Aunt Nell's acreage was home to me. I loved walking around it with her and the dogs, but as the days and weeks passed, I was growing larger and becoming more adventurous. My self confidence increased, until one day I realized, I wasn't a shy, scared, timid little duckling anymore. In fact, I had become a bold, young bird with an enquiring mind.

Chapter Seven

The Good Life

In California, where Aunt Nell lived, there were many different kinds of songbirds that visited her acreage. I saw lots of them when I went into her garden with her to gather fruit and pick ripe veggies. Aunt Nell loved birds and she enjoyed telling me about them. As she pointed out California Scrub Jays, Gold Finches, Mourning Doves and many other kinds of birds. She taught me their names. Every time she saw a bird sitting on a tree branch singing, she would point to it and say, **The little bird twittering over there is a Black Phoebe (or whatever kind of bird it was.) Can you hear the sweet song it is singing to us?**

For example, if it was a meadow lark, she would tell me its name and instruct me to mimic its song. I tried to do this, but I just couldn't get the knack of it. The best I could do was to quack along in time with their songs. Even though I was out of tune, I enjoyed singing with the birds.

I liked how my dear Aunt explained interesting facts about each type in scientific terms, but most of all, I enjoyed learning about Mourning Doves because their soft coo-coo-coos helped me to go to a special peaceful place in my mind. It comforted me and made me feel good. Sometimes I pretended I was a Mourning Dove. When I quacked as low as I could, it sounded like a Mourning Dove with a cold.

One day while I was listening to a Mourning Dove coo, several little Allen's Humming Birds flew into the garden. They were gathering nectar from Aunt Nell's Gooseberry bushes and when Aunt Nell saw them, she asked me if I could hear the song they were singing. This puzzled me because I couldn't hear any singing at all. I cocked my head to one side and stared at Aunt Nell with a puzzled look on my face, as I kicked at the dust with my right foot.

When Aunt Nell saw what I was doing, she laughed and said, *You are right, Ducky. The humming birds are not really singing. What we are hearing is the sound of their tiny wings flapping so fast they vibrate and hum. I can hum and maybe you can hum too.*

After saying this, Aunt Nell started to hum. I liked her humming. It sounded nice. I tried to hum along with her, but all that came out of my mouth was a low, gurgling sound. Nevertheless, it was great fun humming with Aunt Nell and the humming birds, so I just kept right on humming.

On Aunt Nell's property there were many wonderful sights to see. There were also lots of delightful fragrances to smell. I loved waddling around smelling the flowers while Aunt Nell was pulling weeds and so did Whitey and Puppy, even though some of them made us sneeze.

One time, Whitey sniffed a flower with a bee in it. The bee stung Whitey on her shiny, black nose and Whitey ran around in circles yelping with pain and her nose swelled up so much it looked like a balloon. The sight of Whitey running around in circles tickled my funny-bone. I wanted to laugh, but I knew if I did, it would hurt Whitey's feelings, so I stifled my giggles.

That night, when I was alone in the trough, I thought about how funny Whitey had looked with her swollen nose and I chuckled until my sides hurt. What happened that day taught me a valuable lesson and, from then on, I made sure to examine flowers for bees before I smelled them.

During our walks, I usually stayed quite close to Aunt Nell, but one day while Aunt Nell was gathering wild flowers and the dogs were chasing each other through the grass, I struck out on my own.

As I walked along, I noticed a strange animal coming toward me. The animal looked friendly and, as I waddled forward to greet it, I admired its glossy, jet black coat with contrasting snow-white stripes. I was especially fascinated by its big, long, bushy tail! I hoped this animal would be my new playmate. I really wanted him to be my friend, or at least I did until we neared each other and my nose began to sting. He smelled terrible and I shouted, *Pew! Oh pew, pew, pew!* *You stink!*

I thought maybe my prospective new friend was wearing a strange brand of cologne. I was set to tell him to toss that perfume away and choose a different fragrance but I hesitated to do so because I didn't want to offend him. As I stood gagging and trying to make sense of the situation, Whitey raced forward. He zipped past me and came to a screeching halt nose to nose with the handsome stranger.

My black and white new friend did not seem to be upset by Whitey's loud barking. Instead of running away, quick as a flash, he whirled around and with his magnificent tail held high, he squirted poor Whitey square in the face with the nastiest-foulest-smelling liquid ever. After that, he turned and lumbered away, while poor Whitey gagged, spluttered, and ran around in circles yipping and yelping with pain.

By the time Aunt Nell arrived at the scene, the smelly dog was rolling around on the grass whimpering, shaking its head and pawing at its stinging eyes. Aunt Nell took one look at Whitey and said, *Oh, you pitiful animal. You have been sprayed by a skunk. Don't worry. I know what to do. I can help you smell better.*

I clearly recall how Whitey slouched along behind us whimpering and whining with her tail between her legs. I remember that, when we reached the trough, Aunt Nell put me inside it, got into her car, and drove away.

I wondered why Aunt Nell was going for a drive when Whitey was in such a miserable state of pain and despair. She had promised to help poor Whitey, so why wasn't she taking steps to get rid of the terrible odor clinging to Whitey's fur? Why wasn't she doing something to make his eyes stop stinging? I wanted to do something to make Whitey feel better, but I couldn't think of how to help him.

Much to my relief, Aunt Nell was not gone for long. She came home quickly and as soon as she did, she went into her garage. A few minutes later, Aunt Nell came out of her garage carrying the old tin laundry tub. After she set the tub on the ground near Whitey, she went back to her car and carried some sacks to the tub. She placed the sacks beside the tub and walked into her house.

I was puzzled. Why was Aunt Nell not helping Whitey? What was she doing in the house? Had she forgotten about her poor, miserable pooch?

As I pondered these questions, Aunt Nell came out of the house wearing a mask that covered both her nose and mouth. She wore plastic gloves and was carrying a can opener and a tin cup with her. I wondered why she was dressed in such an odd way, and I watched with interest as she opened several cans of tomato juice with the can opener.

After pouring tomato juice into the tub, she lifted Whitey into it and soaked his fur with the juice. Though the tomato juice caused Whitey's coat to turn a beautiful shade of pink, neither Whitey or Aunt Nell seemed to mind it had turned such a charming color. In fact, Whitey seemed to like having a pink coat!

After Aunt Nell rinsed Whitey, she lifted her out of the tub and said, *I know you've been*

31

through a lot. Being bathed with tomato juice isn't fun, but it will do you a world of good.

Aunt Nell was right. Although Whitey had not liked having tomato juice poured all over her, she looked and smelled a lot better than before.

After Whitey was out of the tub, she shook herself and droplets of water flew everywhere. Some of the water splattered on Aunt Nell's clothing and some of it landed on me and we were both soaked. When Aunt Nell and Whitey looked at each other and saw how bedraggled they looked, they both got the giggles… and I did too.

In spite of it being an alarming experience, it was a happy time for us because now, even though Whitey was a pink dog, she surely smelled a lot better.

I hoped Whitey would never again have such a disgusting experience. I was also very sure, if I ever saw another black and white animal coming my way, I would run away from it as fast as I could go!

Chapter Eight
A Close Encounter

The glorious days of summer flew by quickly and each day I was growing a little bit bigger. Every morning (and often several times a day) Aunt Nell lifted me out of the trough and took me exploring. As we walked around the property, I discovered lots of tasty things to eat. My favorite foods were beetles and fat worms. They were really yummy. Sometimes, when a beautiful butterfly flew over my head I would chase after it. It looked like it would be a tasty snack, but I was never able to catch a butterfly so I did not know for sure if it was good to eat.

One day, while I was running after an especially beautiful butterfly, I lost track of where I was. Nothing looked familiar.

Where was I? I was confused and didn't know which way to go. I was lost and upset, so I yelled, *QUA-A-ACK, QUA-A-ACK* (which in duckling talk means: Help! Help! I'm lost.)

When no one responded, I said to myself, Aunt Nell must not have heard me.

I waited for a little while, then I quacked louder and louder over and over again. My throat was getting hoarse from making so much noise and I was almost ready to give up hope of ever being found, when Whitey came running through the tall grass with her nose to the ground.

A wave of relief swept over me, as Whitey ran up to me wagging her tail. I was overjoyed to see her. I was delighted she had found me and I wasn't lost any more.

A few minutes later, Aunt Nell arrived on the scene. It was really good to see her. I was relieved to have been found, and after that, I tried to stay near Aunt Nell when we went walking.

At night I stayed safe in the trough. Then one morning, before Aunt Nell was up, I noticed the lid on my trough was ajar. When I saw this, I said to myself, *If I stand on top of the hay on my tip toes, I will be tall enough to jump up through the opening and go exploring all on my own.*

Feeling bold and fearless, I stood on the hay, flapped my wings as fast as I could, and jumped up toward the opening…and down I came! Although I was disappointed I had not managed to jump through the opening, I remembered what the voice had said to me a long time ago when it encouraged me to keep trying to break out of the shell and I was determined to try again. Filled with fresh energy, I jumped up toward the top of the trough again and again. Each time I jumped, I failed to jump high enough to get out of the trough… until, on my fifth try, I sailed through the opening and landed with a THUD on the ground beside the trough.

Holy Schmoley! Did it ever feel great to be standing outside beside the trough! As I stood there watching the sky turn beautiful shades of pink, gold, orange, and purple, shivers of pleasure surged through me. I wanted to prove I was a brave, fearless duckling. I was itching to go exploring, and I said to myself, *This is my chance to go wherever I choose to go.*

As I strutted along on my adventure, I noticed a path with tracks on it. While examining the tracks, I wondered what kind of animal made them? I was determined to find the answer to my question, so I followed the tracks.

As I waddled along, I imagined I was a great hunter searching for lost treasure. I didn't know where or what it was, but I assumed if I followed the tracks on the path, I would surely find out.

As I skipped along following the tracks, a beautiful monarch butterfly flew over my head. It swooped down close to me several times. Each time it did this, it fluttered swiftly away again. It did this over and over until I lost my focus and followed the butterfly instead of the tracks.

After darting along following the butterfly for several minutes, I realized I couldn't see the path anymore. I remembered how terrible I had felt when I was lost a long time ago. I was now much further away from home than I had been back then and I didn't know what to do.

As I gazed around trying to get my directions, I saw a large animal grazing near a shed, on some lush green grass. I didn't know what kind of an animal it was (though later, I learned it was Aunt Nell's neighbors' bull.)

At first, I did not pay much attention to the bull because I was growing tired and I wondered if I could take a nap in the shed? Maybe there was some hay in the shed and if there was, I could rest on it before I continued trying to find my way home.

I had almost reached the shed, when the animal in the field lifted its head and saw me. It glared at me, snorted loudly, pawed at the ground with its powerful hooves and, all at once, the humongous animal came charging toward me with its big, horny head lowered to the ground.

For a few moments, I stood frozen to the spot with shivers of fear surging through me. I don't know how I managed to regain my composure (maybe it was a miracle?) but I snapped out of my daze and half flying, ran into the shed and hid behind a pile of boards.

I stayed behind the boards for a long time. While there, I could hear the bull banging its head against the shed. Lucky for me, the bull didn't come into the shed. If it had come inside, it probably would have attacked the pile of wood where I was hiding and that would have been the end of me.

Filled with fear, I remained behind that wood until, at last, twilight time arrived and the bull wandered away.

When I left the shed, thank goodness, the bull was nowhere in sight. I wanted to go back to Aunt Nell's place but I didn't know which direction to go in. I was upset and depressed and did not know what to do next until, off in the distance, I heard dogs barking.

"That's Whitey and Puppy!" I yelled, "I'd know their barks anywhere."

As I hurried off in the direction the barking was coming from, I heard Aunt Nell calling my name. I was greatly relieved and thankful, when I saw her and Whitey and Puppy running toward me.

When she reached me, Aunt Nell picked me up and cuddled me close to her chest. I tried to tell her about my adventure, but she still didn't understand duckling talk. Even though Aunt Nell didn't exactly understand what I was saying, she sensed that I'd been through a lot since we had last seen each other.

Where were you, Ducky? said Aunt Nell in a kind and caring tone of voice. I looked all over for you. I was worried. I thought a hawk or an eagle had picked you up and carried you away. Whitey, Puppy, and I have been searching for you for hours. We saw your tracks on a path and we followed them, but after a while, your tracks disappeared. Never mind. I'm just thankful I found you. A coyote or another animal might have caught you and had you for its dinner. Please don't ever run away again. Or at least, don't do it till you can fly fast and high. It's just too dangerous.

While Aunt Nell was talking to me, I gently nibbled on her ear and thanked her in duckling language for her kindness.

When we reached home, Aunt Nell put me back in the trough, but this time, she remembered to firmly secure the lid.

After such a traumatic experience, I was so tired I could hardly waddle up the ramp to the platform. However, I mustered all the energy I could and, when I got there, I gobbled down every bit of my duckling food, jumped onto the hay, stretched out on its comfortable surface, yawned, tucked my curious, imaginative little head under my left wing, and fell sound asleep.

Chapter Nine

Pin Feathers

During my stay in the trough, I learned to be a good swimmer, but the trough was not very large and I longed to swim around in a nice, big pond.

I remembered how, when Aunt Nell first found me, we had gone to a pond where we hoped to find my family. I wanted to go back to that pond and I tried to tell Aunt Nell what I wanted, but she didn't understand a word I said.

Even though Aunt Nell didn't understand me, I kept on cherishing my dream and I often imagined swimming in the big pond. Then, an astonishing thing happened.

One magical day, Aunt Nell came out of the house carrying a bunch of cattails in her hand and said, *These cattails are getting old and scruffy. They are fluffing out and getting lots of fuzzy-wuzzies all over the house. It's time to toss them into the trash and gather some fresh, new cattails.*

Aunt Nell went on to tell me she had noticed what a good swimmer I had become. She told me I was now capable of swimming in the big pond and she would take me there.

I was happy and excited. My wish was coming true. I was going to the pond with Aunt Nell and I could hardly wait to get there, so I waddled up to Aunt Nell and impatiently tugged with my bill on her skirt.

Okay, Ducky, okay, said Aunt Nell. Give me a few minutes to pack a lunch for us to take with us. After I get the lunch made, we will go to the big pond.

It did not take Aunt Nell long to pack our lunch and after it was ready, we set out to walk to the pond. I felt confident as we strolled along, for in the past few weeks I had grown a lot and become much stronger. I now had enough energy to walk all the way to the big pond without becoming tired.

As soon as we arrived at the pond, I plunged into the water and swam around to my heart's content splashing and chasing bugs. I flapped my wings in the water and beautiful rainbow-hued drops of water flew high. Ah, what fun! Joy oh joy! This was the life and I was enjoying every minute of it.

Because I was so excited and delighted with my activities, I paid no attention to Aunt Nell while she picked fresh cattails. In fact, I was so busy having fun, I lost track of time and it came as a surprise when she called out, **Ducky, come here. It's lunch time.**

I was reluctant to stop swimming and take time out for lunch, so I told Aunt Nell, in duck talk, I wasn't hungry. I explained this was because I was enjoying eating as many swift, little water bugs as I could catch.

Aunt Nell must have understood part of what I said, because she did not insist I come out of the water. Instead, she finished her lunch and said, *I can see you have been snacking on water bugs, so I won't need to bring any duckling food with me the next time we come here. But Ducky, we must go home immediately. Look at the sky! It is as black as pitch. A big rainstorm is coming.*

I had been so busy swimming and playing in the pond, I had not noticed how dark the sky had become. I was surprised when I looked up and saw several bright sparks of lightning zigzagging through the sky. Immediately after the lightning flashed, a tremendously loud bang- bang-bang of thunder roared. This scared me and I scurried out of the pond and ran to Aunt Nell.

When Aunt Nell saw how frightened I was, she scooped me up, held me close to her chest and carried me home.

Going to the big pond had been a magical experience for me and I hoped, in the future, we would go there every day. And guess what… we did. Well… to be truthful… we went there **almost** every day.

Each time we went to the pond, Aunt Nell carried a folding chair with her and, upon arriving at the pond, she sat down on the chair with her feet dangling in the water. When the sun shined on the water, Aunt Nell's toenails glistened. I enjoyed dipping under the water so I could nibble on them. Every time I nibbled on Aunt Nell's toenails, she giggled, closed the book she was reading, relaxed, and simply enjoyed being outside in the sunshine. Aunt Nell's toenails were not the only things I liked to nibble on. Sometimes, when Aunt Nell was holding me on her lap. I also nibbled on her long, glossy braid.

One day when Aunt Nell was sitting on her chair with her feet in the water, holding me on her lap stroking my back, she suddenly exclaimed, ***PIN-FEATHERS!*** *Oh my stars! Ducky, you are growing pin-feathers! This means it won't be long until you are able to fly high into the sky!*

I was startled by what she said. I gravely doubted I would ever be able to fly very high. However, as I pondered the thought of flying through the air, I very much liked the idea and I said to myself, *Maybe Aunt Nell is right. When I grow a whole bunch of pin-feathers, I really will be able to soar through the sky.*

As the days sped by, I grew lots of new feathers and my downy baby duck fluff disappeared. I also learned to preen my new feathers. I didn't know anything about preening until the time I discovered an itchy bump near my backside and poked at it with my bill. I rubbed my bill into the oil and spred it from my bill onto my brand new feathers. After I did this, my feathers began to shine. I liked having shiny, waterproof feathers, so I proudly preened and polished my feathers every day.

When it rained, I would have loved to go down to swim in the big pond but Aunt Nell didn't go out at that time. Instead, she stayed in her house and her two dogs snuggled up in their doghouse, while I strutted around outside in the yard, splashing in puddles with the rain pouring down on me. I loved walking in the rain because, since I had learned to preen, the raindrops rolled off my feathers like 'water on a duck's back' and I didn't get soaked to my skin.

While out walking on those rainy days, there were lots of angle worms squirming around in the mud. I loved how they tasted and I ate as many of them as my tummy could hold. They reminded me of one of Aunt Nell's favorite foods… spaghetti! I enjoyed pretending I was eating spaghetti when I was really slurping down worms.

Although I liked rainy days, I liked sunny days even better. I liked them because when the weather was nice and warm, I often got to swim in the big pond. Aunt Nell also enjoyed being at the big pond, so the four of us (Aunt Nell, Whitey, Puppy, and me) spent a lot of time there.

Aunt Nell knew how happy I was when I was swimming in the big pond. She also understood how proud I was of my new feathers, but she did not know that I had a secret. She never guessed how every time we went to the pond, I wished my egg-laying mother or some of my brothers or sisters would be at the pond waiting for me. But they never were. I was always the only duck swimming in the pond. That is. I was always the only one, until one fine morning when we reached the pond, four attractive ducks were gracefully swimming around in the water.

I was so excited. At last I was going to meet my family! However, I had always thought my family would look like me, but these four ducks didn't look much like me at all. They were larger than me and had shining, beautiful, many-coloured feathers all over their bodies.

At that time, I only had a few dozen pin-feathers mixed in with my baby fluff. The few real feathers coming in, were a very plain motley brown color. I figured I must have looked quite unappealing to the handsome green-headed ducks. Oh how I wished I had a dazzling green head like their heads! But I didn't. As I studied my reflection in the water, I could see I was not half as pretty as they were.

I might have been discouraged when I realized this, but when I noticed my bill was the same color as their bills, I decided it didn't matter much if my feathers were not very beautiful. I reasoned, since our bills were the same color, we at least had something in common.

Though it took me a few hours to size things up and overcome my natural shyness, my self confidence came back and I swiftly paddled toward the ducks on the other side of the pond. I was tremendously eager to make friends with those four fine looking feathered fellows, but when they saw me coming, they swam toward me at great speed with their necks stretched out toward me and a mean gleam in their eyes. When they reached me, three of the ducks began to bite me with their strong bills. Even though they didn't have teeth like a lot of animals do, their bites were painful. All that pinching hurt and I did not like it at all. Their angry actions disappointed me and I didn't know what to do.

A few minutes passed before I got over the shock of their rudeness and I said to myself, *I had better get out of here. These ducks are not friendly at all. They don't want me near them. I think they are warning me to stay on my side of the pond or else!*

I quickly turned around and swam as fast as I could back to my side of the pond. The ducks did not follow me. Instead, they swam back to their side of the pond and, as long as I stayed on my side of the pond, they left me alone.

I wondered why only three of the ducks had bitten me? I did not know why the other duck had not bitten me too. I thought perhaps he was better natured than the others. Being bitten by three of those rascals had been bad enough.

After that, each time Aunt Nell and I and the dogs came home from the big pond, I made a point of practicing my flying skills. At first things did not go well. Each time I jumped up onto a large stone and tried to fly off it, I ended up landing on the ground with a thud. However I kept on practicing and before long, I was finally able to fly for a few minutes at a time!

Chapter Nine
A Love Story

During my first months of life, things had gone well for me. While living with Aunt Nell, I was a happy, satisfied duckling. My beloved Aunty was always kind to me. I loved her and I couldn't have asked for a better mommy. She filled my feed bowl every day and I had a nice bed of hay to sleep on at night, though now that I could fly, I hardly ever slept in my trough any more. Instead, I slept in a cozy, safe spot under Aunt Nell's back porch. I was comfortable there, and each evening after the sun went down, I crept under the porch and didn't come out from under it till early the next day. Sometimes I got up before Aunt Nell did in order to practice flying and it was not long before I could half fly and half-waddle down to the big pond in almost no time at all. On the days I went to the pond alone, I was careful to stay on my side of the pond so the four big ducks wouldn't bother me.

Even though my initial meeting with those four had not gone well, I still enjoyed observing them as they swam and dived into the water with their bottoms pointing up ward toward the sun. One day, when Aunt Nell was there too, she told me they were Drake Mallards. She said this meant they were boy ducks. She explained to me I was not a drake duck. Instead, I was a little Hen Mallard which meant I was a girl duck that would one day lay eggs and when my eggs hatched I would become a Mother Duck.

As Aunt Nell was telling me this, I cocked my head to one side and looked at her with a puzzled expression. When Aunt Nell saw how perplexed I was, she smiled and said, *You must be wondering how I know you are a female duck. Well, the truth is, I didn't, or at least I didn't until your new feathers appeared. When you were about 7 weeks old and your new feathers started growing in, I saw they were a nice, soft, speckled brown. That's how I knew you were a hen and not a drake. Drakes may have fancier feathers than you do, but they certainly don't have as good of a voice as you do. Their voices are low and gravelly and they can't quack nearly as clearly as you can. I am a female human being. Puppy and Whitey are female dogs and you are a female duck. We are an all girl family. Isn't that nice?*

I liked Aunt Nell's explanation and even though my being a girl duck meant my feathers were not as attractive as the boy ducks' feathers were, I was happy I was a girl. By then, I could fly as well as the four drakes and, now that my feathers were fully grown, the other ducks seemed more friendly. I didn't know why, but maybe it was because I was not afraid to show off my skills?

It must have surprised the four male drakes when they saw me flying faster and higher than they did. I only know I was proud of myself and it didn't matter to me if they were better looking than I was. I had proved a point to them and from that time on, they admired me as I swam around on my side of the pond.

Actually, they not only admired me, they did all kinds of silly things to get my attention. I wondered if they were competing with each other to see which one of them I liked best.

When October rolled around, I noticed the boy ducks' heads were getting greener than ever and the greener they got, the more tricks they did. It was entertaining to watch them lift their wings to show off the bright blue patches of feathers beneath their wings. Sometimes I lifted my wings to show them I too had a few pretty blue patches under my wings.

In particular, I liked one of the tricks they did. It amused me greatly when they bobbed their heads rapidly back and forth and dived down into the water with their bottoms above the water and their tails pointing straight up into the air. I knew something had changed and by the end of October, I was daily taking flights with the drakes.

As we flew through the sky together, Aunt Nell watched us with tears in her eyes. Later, she told me she knew I was growing up. She said if I ever wanted to go away with the drakes, she would miss me but she wouldn't stop me from going. She spoke to me about freedom. She said freedom of choice was my natural right and she would honor all my choices. She assured me, if I always listened to the voice of my heart when I made a decision, things would work out for the best.

A few times, I thought the drakes were going to leave the pond forever. I supposed they were going to go away and live somewhere else. Sometimes I would fly with them for a little while, but before I got far, I would think of Aunt Nell and Whitey and Puppy. Then I would fly back and spend the night sleeping under the porch. In the morning, I'd return to the pond and find the drakes waiting for me.

One fine morning when I flew to the pond, only one drake was there. He was the one that had not bitten me when we first met. When he saw me, he started performing tricks. He even caught a small fish and gave it to me for my breakfast. I was impressed with his kindness and, as I gobbled it down, I knew he was my one and only.

As I watched with amazement, my drake stretched his head straight up into the air and for the first time in his life, he whistled! I had never had anyone whistle at me before and it made me feel beautiful.

I sighed and said to myself, *Yep, he's the one for me! His plumage is brighter than the plumages of the other drakes. He does tricks better than any of them. For sure, he's my one and only.*

Immediately after I thought these things, the other three drakes showed up. When they realized my drake and I were swimming side by side close to each other, they concluded we had become mates and they flew away.

As we watched them disappear from sight, my drake nudged me. I knew he wanted us to fly away with them, but I hesitated because I knew if I went with him, I might never see Aunt Nell and the dogs again. Then I remembered what Aunt Nell had told me about freedom and about listening to my heart.

As I was thinking things over, my handsome drake stretched his head straight up into the air and whistled again. After that, he flapped his wings and soared high into the bright, blue sky. And guess what? I flew into the air right along with him!

Today, I treasure the memory of the last time I saw Aunt Nell, Whitey, and Puppy. In my mind's eye, I can still see them standing beside the barn gazing up at us, as my drake and I soared through the air. I still clearly recall the smile on Aunt Nell's face and the tears in her eyes, as she watched us go.

I will never forget Aunt Nell. I will always miss her.

Even though I now have twelve newly hatched ducklings to look after, I think of Aunt Nell often. The love in my heart for this precious lady forever remains as fresh and sweet as it was on the day I flew away.

AUNT NELL'S
Dandy Duckling

An orphaned wild duckling tells the true story of how she goes searching for her mother after breaking free from her shell and finding herself alone. Instead of finding her mother, the plucky little bird encounters a kindly lady who adopts her and looks after her. In spite of experiencing many challenges, the dandy duckling has fun growing up on Aunt Nell's acreage, or at least, she does, until her heart hears a strange and tantalizing eerie call.

A. L. Kirby grew up on a spacious cattle ranch in Southern Alberta, Canada, where she spent her childhood enjoying nature's beauty and wonders. Life blessed A. L. and her husband with six children, fifteen grandchildren, and two great-grandchildren. A. L. is the author of two published, illustrated children's books and a full-length script about a little indigenous girl, which she hopes will one day become a family movie. A. L. also loves writing poetry and has written hundreds of poems.

Milton Keynes UK
Ingram Content Group UK Ltd.
UKHW051701221024
449870UK00005B/11